The Hedge Witch & The Magical Poet

Poems & Flash Fiction

MJ Mallon

Manuscript Prepared by Unicorn Cats Publishing Services

Paperback ISBN: 978-1-9998224-7-7

Published in kindle, and paperback

Cover Design and formatting by: Unicorn Cats Publishing Services

mjmallon.com

THE HEDGE WITCH & THE MAGICAL POET

Dedication

To my mum and dad, my daughters, hubby, my family, and friends. You are so dear to my heart. Here's to precious days spent in the forest's beauty. And to the trees, there would be no words, and no poetry without your beauty.

Foreward

This book is a wondrous celebration of the forest, woodland, natural world, the trees, and the many creatures who live within its realms. Many of the poems are inspired by my experiences, or by observations I have made.

The Scorched Tree is a poignant reminder of the rising problems of global warming, the sad destruction of trees caused by a forest fire in Portugal. I wasn't there when it happened, but I witnessed the aftermath, and it was devastating to see.

The Trees Debating is a personal anecdote, the sad removal of part of the forest which I played in as a child, in my old hometown of Edinburgh. My father, who has been a resident there since he was a child, complained to the local council, but unfortunately, residents' pleas fell on deaf ears. Sadly, some of the beautiful woodland was destroyed to make way for new houses.

The Anger of The Orangutans brings back memories of a frightening experience in the Malaysian Jungle when my aunt, uncle, mother, daughters, and I were told to run for our lives!

"Orangutans are the largest arboreal mammal, spending most of their time in trees. Known for their distinctive red fur, orangutans are the largest arboreal mammal, spending most of their time in trees. Found only on the islands of Borneo and Sumatra, Asia's only great apes are rapidly losing their forest homes to oil palm and other agricultural plantations. Today, more than 50% of orangutans are found outside protected areas in forests under management by timber, palm oil and mining companies."

(Source: https://www.worldwildlife.org/stories/10-species-that-hug-trees)

Chester, Don, and I share the tale of my Edinburgh tomcat, Chester. He used to get up to all sorts of mischief. And often, he went off on some grand adventure to socialise! One time, my brother Donald and I scrambled through the forest on our way to pick him up from a nearby location. He'd ended up at a house with thirteen cats, so of course he liked it there!

There's a section about holiday homes in forest places, a nostalgic looking back to the days when we used to go to Centre Parcs, where holiday makers enjoyed the forest for short periods of time, unplugging from modern life. On one such trip, our youngest daughter, Georgina had an asthma attack. It was her birthday, and she was so excited to be there! Luckily, she was okay and recovered to enjoy the holiday.

Two of the poems are about my mum and dad's experiences whilst up a tree: *Mum Climbing Trees*, and *Two Boys Watching War*. My mum used to love climbing trees as a youngster, growing up in Kuching, Malaysia.

My dad climbed a tree with his friend, JG Adamson, (Adie) in Edinburgh, Scotland. Whilst up the tree, the two boys witnessed Spitfires on their way towards the Firth of Forth.

"It was the 16th October 1939 - The Battle of The River Forth between Supermarine Spitfires from No. 602 and No. 603 Squadrons of the Royal Air Force and Junkers Ju 88 bombers of 1. It resulted when twelve Ju 88s attacked Rosyth naval base at the Firth of Forth. This was the first German air raid on Britain during World War II."

(Source: Wikipedia, https://wiki2.org/en/Battle_of_the_River_Forth)

I've added a Halloween poem I wrote some time ago, which I've rewritten for this collection, entitled *All Hallows Eve, Candy Girl*. I love writing Halloween poems!

There are some additional poems which were originally featured in my poetry, prose, and photography collection: *Mr. Sagittarius Poetry and Prose*: *Dreaming at Halloween, A Face on Bark: Etheree, Golden Willow Tree, Rainbow, Parasol of Light and Lollipop Sunshine Tree*, which seemed appropriate to include in this collection.

The final section is inspired by various poets: Henry Wadsworth Longfellow, Ruby Archer, Bliss Carman, Emily Dickinson, Rupert Blake, Oscar Wilde, and their lovely forest poems, which I have reinterpreted.

All the poems are a tribute to the beauty of the trees, the forest, the jungle and natural habitats, including a dear wish that we shall preserve them for our children and children's children.

M J Mallon

Contents

The Hedge Witch & The Musical Poet

A man staggers ahead, dragging his feet,

Blood dripping from the cuts on his face.

Wiping his eyes, he discerns a clearing ahead,

With flowers, trees, and the hum of insects.

Unable to walk any further, he collapses by a tree.

His hands reach out to touch the earth,

And water drops from the river trickle,

Over his bruised fingertips.

Outside, a forest cabin, a girl wanders,

Her hands are dirty from digging in her garden.

Worms wiggle at her feet,

While above her plentiful bees fly from flower to flower,

Collecting nectar.

She pauses for a moment,

To sit on a bench with her forest friends,

Who often greet her.

A robin joins her,

His presence warms her heart,

As she studies his plump red breast,

Grey under belly, brown head, wings, and tail.

The robin flits to and fro.

Flying in short bursts of flight,

He doesn't settle beside her as it usually does.

"What's wrong robin?" she asks.

Placing her hand out in a gentle gesture,

Of kind friendship,

She is surprised to see,

That the robin doesn't come to rest on her hand,

As he normally does.

Instead, he lands on her shoulder,

And gently tugs at the fabric of her dress,

As if urging her to come with him.

"Okay, okay," she says,

As she follows him into the forest.

The robin flies with rapid wing beats.

She follows, from time-to-time the bird pauses,

To check that she is still there.

At last, he stops to rest,

At the edge of the forest, by a river,

By the weeping willow tree.

He chooses this place to land,

On a branch,

That rests still in the water.

Beside the branch there is a man prone,

His face squashed in the dirt.

The weeping willow tree bends its branches,

Reaching towards the injured man,

As if the man might reach out.

And be helped to his feet.

The injured man's eyes open momentarily,

He tries to grasp the tree branch,

But he is too weak to do so.

The Willow's branches sway to and fro.

Scattering,

Droplets,

Of water on his battered face...

Rushing over, the young woman's heart beats with worry as she comes to the man's aid. Bending down, she turns his face, removes the dirt from his mouth, presses her ear to his chest and listens to see if he is breathing. His breathing sounds laboured. She frowns with worry, knowing that she must get him to her cottage. Fast. But how?

Amongst the foliage, she notices her friend the deer peering out inquisitively. The creature pads towards her and stops.

"Deer, can you help me? I must awaken this hurt creature without delay and take him to my cottage to tend its wounds."

The deer sniffs the air, its eyes wide with understanding.

The deer moves towards the man, sniffing him, licking the man's face, washing him with tender licks of concern. The willow's branches sway a little in the wind splashing droplets of water on his face. The girl waits with the robin, who sits in her palm, her hand resting on the robin's beating heart.

The deer's licking action seems to revive him.

He groans, muttering, "Where am I?"

"You are in the forest by the weeping willow tree. Let me help you stand up," she replies.

The man accepts her help, and she supports his weight as much as she can on the way to her cottage. The deer and the robin follow their progress. They stop and rest and continue again. As they walk, nearby flower heads open, their petals unfurling with curiosity, while the fungi clump together in circles, gossiping.

She opens the door to her cottage, a simple home fashioned out of wood. It is decorated with natural fibres, hand carved wooden owls, spirits, and wind chimes. Its many open shuttered windows let in an abundance of bright, illuminating light. There is an altar with crystals, a triple moon tea light candle holder fashioned out of wood, and one made of salt.

She helps him in. He moans, his eyes closed tight with the pain. Glancing over to her bedroom door, she smiles a little, relieved to see she has left the door open. With some difficulty, she eases him onto the bed. She rearranges his position as best she can and with a gentle tug; she removes his muddy boots.

Rushing to the kitchen, her lace-up boots pound the wooden floor of her cottage, an unfamiliar sound in the everyday tranquillity, as tiny beads of sweat drip down her brow. She fills a bowl full of warm water filled with freshly picked aromatic rose flower petals and brings a face cloth to wash his bloodied face.

There are colourful bruises around his mouth and jaw. She touches these with tender fingertips, fearful to hurt him further. Shocked by these deep and painful injuries, tears fall from her eyes. While he rests, she makes up a healing poultice of yarrow, calendula, and witch hazel to tend to his wounds, as she chants a healing spell.

Power of light, keep this man from harm,

power bright, mirrored light,

keep this man safe and well with your magic insight.

Heal, restore, heal restore him!

Over the next few days, she cares for him, day and night, not bothering to sleep. The girl meditates, visualising him getting well. She treats his wounds, and makes powerful healing and protective concoctions of garlic, cinnamon, rosemary, and bay leaf to make him strong. She fills the room with transforming, powerful and healing crystals: malachite, black tourmaline, fluorite, bloodstone, jasper, and places a burner by his bedside, omitting the healing aroma of tea tree and orange.

When he is well enough to speak, he asks, "Where am I?"

She doesn't know how to answer. There are places beyond this forest. Cities, towns, bustling locations, places she has never visited. This is her home, the forest of life.

She lived here with her mother, Agnes, but her mother died long ago, when she was a young girl, of a terrible affliction that even her herbs and magic could not heal.

Her life is simple. She fishes in the river for food, collecting wild mushrooms, foraging for berries and fruit. She spends plentiful hours tending to the vegetables and herbs in her cottage garden. The birds and animals in the forest are her only friends. Her rosy, freckled face exudes happiness, and her long brown hair shines with lighter strands bleached by the sun.

She peers at this creature, who is so like her, but so different. "What creature are you?" she asks. Her voice is quiet and trembles a little with fear.

"Creature?" he replies, his eyes wide. "I am no creature. I am a man, a human, and you are a human woman."

"No human man has ever stumbled upon this magical hidden forest before. I have never seen your like before."

Struck by his beauty, his wide shoulders, dark brown hair and warm brown eyes, these handsome attributes bring a blush of heightened colour to her cheeks. A strange dance stirs in her belly as she looks at him. She shyly looks away, unable to cope with this depth of feeling that she has never experienced before.

"Who are you? What is your name?" he asks, raising his heavy head, confused.

"I'm Fern," she replies, smiling.

"Where am I? I..." he attempts to sit up but cannot do so. With a groan, his head sinks back into the pillow.

"Take care. You must not exhaust yourself. You must rest."

His eyes become dark pools of distress, inky black like she has never seen before. For a moment she steps back, looking for her forest friends to protect her.

"I'm sorry. I don't mean to frighten you. Let me explain. I was thinking about what happened. I was at the local pub..."

Her eyes widen with confused curiosity.

"Oh, I see. You don't know what a pub is. A pub is a place where you go for a drink. You pay for the drink and enjoy the company of friends."

She nods and waits for him to continue.

"This man, a stranger, provoked an argument with me. By mistake, I spilled beer on him."

"What is beer?"

"It is an alcoholic beverage which makes you light-headed and jolly. But some people react badly to too much of it. This man became angry, punching me. I staggered out, trying to get away, but he kept on following me with his fist. I must have blanked out."

"Why would someone do such a horrible thing to you? Is this alcohol a demon?" her eyes widen with a look of horrified concern, as if she has never heard of such violence before.

"No demon. Some people don't need much to become aggressive. It is commonplace where I come from. Fights, trouble, especially in big cities. Where is this cottage? It is so different, so calm and tranquil."

"I live at the edge of mankind's kingdom in this enchanted forest, in Misty Willow Wood. I hail from a long line of hedge witches."

His eyes grow wide with fear at her words. He attempts to push himself up from the bed, as he exclaims, "You're a witch!"

"Don't fear, I am a gentle witch, one with healing powers. I have never harmed a soul." She lays a gentle hand on his broad shoulder.

Too weak to argue or resist, she helps him sit up and smiles a sweet smile. "I'll be right back."

She returns with the healing water she has made, which she shakes gently. The bubbles fill the glass and keep on coming.

His eyes widen in surprise.

"Try some," she urges.

"Is it safe?"

"Of course it is," she smiles.

His lips touch the glass as he drinks. He chokes as the bubbles tickle the back of his throat.

"Drink slowly," she urges. "I infused this water with great power. Take small sips. What is your name, human man?"

"I... I can't remember," he replies, as he sips.

"It doesn't matter," she says. With two drops of water, she anoints his forehead. "You are now Devin, which means musical poet. When you are well, you will play and write, and thereafter your heart will sing."

Over the next few days, Devin's health improves. He becomes well enough to sit at the table with her. By the end of the week, she takes him for short walks in the forest, clutching his hand to keep him safe. He marvels at the beauty and majesty of the magnificent trees, fragrant flowers, and plentiful plants.

Within a week, she encourages him to take an important walk. She fashions a walking stick made from silver birch to help Devin in case he grows weak on his long way there. From the beginning, she knew that she must take him to pay his respects to the willow tree.

The deer and the robin come too. As they walk, many creatures, birds and insects of the forest follow them, and a beautiful butterfly with shimmering wings lands on Devin's shoulder as they arrive.

"The Willow is beautiful," he remarks, his breath somewhat laboured from his exertion; but he smiles.

The willow tree's branches sway towards him as if responding to his kind remark.

"This is where I gather the healing water. It is said that the tears of heaven fall and kiss the willow's branches."

Fern moves towards Devin, who is now leaning heavily on the walking stick. "Let me help you," she says.

She reaches out to him, tucking her arms through his. He smiles and his eyes twinkle. The branches of the willow tree move towards them, nuzzling them towards each other.

Devin's eyes twinkle as he pulls Fern towards him, and he bends down as she reaches up to kiss him. Their lips meet in a sweet kiss as the robin cocks its head and the deer bows, pretending to sniff the ground at its feet.

All around them, the forest creatures witness the joining of the hedge witch with the musical poet. Silence encircles them. The rustle of the tree leaves, the only sound to be heard. Thereafter, this is accompanied by the sound of music and words which fill the air - a natural melody of joy.

The joined pair remain locked in their sweet embrace for a long time. When they draw apart, Devin is so overwhelmed by his emotions that he weeps.

"Why are you crying?" she asks, her eyes wide in surprise.

"I am so happy," he replies.

"When we are happy, we smile. Hedge witches weep when another creature dies."

He wipes away his tears and smiles a beautiful smile that brings an intense rainbow of light and joy that fills the forest with light.

He recites a love poem to her, and his voice sounds like an instrument, a perfect instrument of love.

> *Love is a starry day with you,*
>
> *dazzling moonlight paths,*
>
> *tender drops of rain falling,*
>
> *illuminating smiles.*
>
> *Love is the forest and us,*
>
> *our sweet love growing,*
>
> *just like the sun's rays bring light,*
>
> *illuminating joy.*

Rain Forest Love

In the moonlight,

a young woman dances naked,

the forest senses her plight,

as the clouds fill, she prays for a lover,

to touch her as tenderly as the rain,

to her surprise, her wish is fulfilled.

One day, a stranger comes,

he draws her to him with such passion

she sighs, soon the forest will have

a new babe to cradle.

A Forest Baby Boy
(Reversed Etheree)

a forest witch has had a baby boy

Rory, he belongs to the forest

to his parents Devin and Fern

together they live in joy

Rory will learn to walk

he will climb a tree

he'll catch moonbeams

sun kissed be

raindrops

joy

A Forest Baby Girl (Etheree)

now

he has

a sister,

Kate is her name

she is so naughty

everyone laughs, loves her

how she brings forest mischief

the trees sway with mirth and rustle

but they protect her too, keep her safe

she is a kin of the forest, that's why

A Modern Witch

A modern witch is a curious being,

a beautiful child of autumn,

never winter's babe, never old,

she breathes in spells,

and speaks with wisdom.

But often sits alone in whimsy,

in crowded places,

remembering ancient times, she muses,

thoughts when truth was real,

and witches feared and killed.

In long queues, she waits, pondering,

on the bus, she stares out the window,

until at home, she bakes zucchini bread,

paints long, never polished nails,

and keeps a sleek, black cat.

She's like you in many ways,

but yet, some say, "not all!"

Her heart longs for ancient songs to sing,

rainy days and forest moonlit nights,

unifying treasured ways.

One day by chance she finds a book,

as burnt and blackened as dust,

resting in an old knot of a tree root,

forgotten, abandoned,

she takes it home.

Upon its charred pages,

torn words sing, forgotten forest songs,

in every turn of its crumbling pages,

she finds a happiness and a way to be,

a witch in a frantic, modern world.

Rock of Mine

In the forest, there is a rock

a lone rock that shines.

I dare not pass the rock by,

so, I crouch contemplating,

its many polished surfaces.

So sublime, rock of old.

Yet I neglect to touch you,

or sit upon you, rock.

No, I just stare and wait,

wait, for what I do not know.

I fear one day I will weaken,

I will succumb, climb upon you,

and tumble to my knees.

So, I remain locked here,

at a safe distance.

Just watching, waiting,

feeling your weakness within.

Don't break, beautiful rock,

my childhood friend,

dear rock, stay strong.

Chester, Don & I

A flash of ginger fur,

blurred in vast woodland,

I see you,

Chester—

Cat of Kings.

Some cats are made for...

grand adventures,

making new friends,

causing mischief,

creating mayhem.

Donald and I,

trudged through these woods,

to find you, you rascal!

MJ MALLON

Where might you be?

A house with thirteen cats, perhaps?

Thirteen cats with all unique personalities,

but my ginger tomcat,

little Chester, once a kitten

tiny, playful, such a cutie.

Stole, and kept my heart.

What were you up to?

Playing out, were you?

Did you find new human friends?

My friendly fellow,

I miss you, still.

Every day.

I do.

The Network of Trees

The network of trees were debating terrible news.

"What?" they clamoured," shake, rattling their branches.

The forest is to be destroyed!

No! No!

The young saplings trembled and cried, "How can this be? No!

New houses are needed, so we must make way!"

Felled, forgotten, forever.

The old humans who once played as children in our branches,

they don't stand a chance; their cries go ignored!

You know how things are,

no one cares for the forest anymore,

or the wisdom of the elderly.

The old are pushed aside.

Our present is the forgotten past.

The trees debated what to do next...

So, are we ancients, to be replaced by bricks,

garages, cars, bicycles, people?

A small play area, no trees? Not one!

The trees' declarations couldn't be heard.

The furious dryads were mocked.

The birds flapped their wings in a fit of fury,

no one moved—least of all the trees.

The trees steeled their bark,

wise and proud until the bitter end,

such is the will of the forest,

the melancholy heart of the trees will remain.

More Trees Not Less

Dear neighbours,

we need trees to be planted,

to grow and be cared for,

dig deep, choose wisely,

watch them grow.

Reforestation is needed,

six times more,

in England alone.

Up above, view a canopy of deciduous hardwood trees,

shrubs in the middle,

down below, ferns, sedges, fungi, wildflowers, moss,

lichen and insects.

We need trees everywhere

to improve air quality,

water infiltration,

for shading in our ever-warming climate,

to protect against flash flooding.

Two Boys Watching War

Two boys watching war, making up stories.

Dad climbed a tree with his friend Adie. They pointed as the Spitfires flew past, staring, fascinated, wondering what would happen next.

Two boys watching war, making up stories.

Now eighty-three years later, Dad remembers that tree and that day, the tree is gone, but not forgotten. The horrors of war remain an indelible memory.

War is still seen, felt, and suffered by children, and all such horrors are to be lamented forever.

Mum Climbing Trees

My mum loved to climb trees,

up in the top branches, she would stay,

watching her world from a distance,

enjoying the freedom she found,

up in their leafy, lofty branches.

There she could snatch time,

be alone for a while,

think her own thoughts,

while below, animals passed by,

a dog perhaps, a goose, or even a cobra!

Let's Play

No one plays in the forest anymore.

It's a silent place, where once it was a land of adventure,

the children stay at home on their computers,

tap-tapping their mobile phones—

the children are safe inside.

The trees want the children back.

They long for them to play in their branches,

they wish to hear their childhood cries,

as they imagine their games with twigs and branches,

but the children are safe inside.

No one can live without adventure,

try this, climb that, gaze skywards,

see the moon shining above,

catch a star and scoop it up.

But the children are safe inside.

Scramble up a tree's branches,

steal a leaf, pop it in your pocket,

deep down in the warm lining, keep it safe,

Until the next time, a new shiny leaf.

Now, the children are safe outside.

The Scorched Tree

The scorched earth, blackened bark—

forest fire.

Why here? Why now?

No answers, only questions.

Time to act was yesterday.

See the black finger of fury pointing at you...

The scorched tree, blackened bark—

forest fire.

Right here, right now!

Questions and answers,

too late for this charcoal reminder.

The death of this young tree.

Owl's Holiday Home

An owl resting in the branches grew tired,

his eyes closing,

unable to hoot, he hailed a cab,

to the nearest forest holiday home.

An owl's resting place for the ancient,

in this tree,

witches are welcome too!

A Man's Holiday Home

A man in his home grew restless,

his eyes opening and closing,

unable to rest, he hailed a cab,

to the nearest forest holiday home.

A human place for the overworked,

Family is welcome too!

A Child's Excitement!

A child so excited she can't breathe,

her chest rising and falling,

so much to do, so much fun,

in the nearest forest holiday home.

Too much excitement for the childhood asthmatic,

her family will help her breathe!

The Teddy in The Woods

There is a shack in the woods, an old tumble-down ruin.

Visitors pass by unaware of its history.

If you walk in, you will find an old chair, table, and a broken picture frame.

The aroma of lavender still lingers.

On the table stands a vase,

filled with muddy water where fresh flowers once bloomed.

In the far corner, a teddy bear sits contemplating life,

his one good eye remembering...

the little girl who once lived here,

who's now grown up,

and moved away.

Run! The Orangutans!

"Run," the guide yelled. "The orangutans are riled. They are protecting their young. Run!"

We didn't stop to think. We ran through the jungle with the blistering heat and the enraged anger of the orangutans biting on our heels.

My aunt, the fittest and fastest led, followed by my youngest daughter. We didn't dare to look back. I ran but wasn't fast. But I was fast enough.

Gasping, we made it. The rage of the Orangutans, a fearful but justified memory, remembered as our breathing settled down.

All Hallows Eve Candy Girl

The Forest Bash

Curvaceous candy stick girl,

her brash hair bright pink,

her nails dark as ink,

she sashays by and disappears—

a tickled-pink apparition.

Dressed in rainbow stripy stockings

she teases with her lipstick smile,

twirls by too darn quick,

like champagne bubbles,

blinking through false lashes. See.

A passerby's hair is dark lollipop-blue

nails a pretty sky hue,

caught enjoying sweet nibbles,

she sighs, candy-lipped,

her sensual silks sway.

In symphonies of sweet organza,

bubblegum hearts steal,

sugar sweet babes,

licorice, all-sorts.

Let's sashay away, marshmallows.

Too tempting not to taste.

Trick or treat, sugar-tipped,

coins, gum, pick and mixes,

chewy, jelly, sherbet fixes,

candy cone bites mingle.

As Joker snatches bonbon handfuls

devils desire red chilli sweets,

vampire fangs dipped in space dust,

pumpkin gobstoppers abound,

Addams family—Cousin It.

Who sits with VIP scary magic minx's,

witches, and sugar twitches,

cocktail umbrellas and alcohol pitchers,

the woodland party heightens and revels,

trick or tricksters tumble from trees.

Into sugar-coated fern ditches.

Ghostly gatecrasher's senses tremble.

One chocolate heart is never enough!

Skeletons, please... die, resuscitate,

come back for one last forest fizzing bite!

Dreaming At Halloween

I dream in colour,

but now everything is murky,

where has the light gone?

Oh, cruel leafy canopy,

no green meadow, just blue thoughts.

A spectre haunts me,

through the trees, he approaches

I hear no weeping,

just a tall, grey wall of sighs,

twigs snap, and nothing changes.

(This poem originally appeared in *Mr. Sagittarius Poetry and Prose*.)

A Face on Bark (Etheree)

I

see you

in the trees

a face in bark,

your sad love-me look

the way nature moved you

my dear champion, darling,

giant man, never forgotten,

colossal reach beyond desire.

a network of roots brings me to your heart.

(This poem originally appeared in *Mr. Sagittarius Poetry and Prose*)

Golden Willow Tree

So charming you are

Sweet golden willow bending

Longing for water

Not I, deep depths frighten me

I long to touch you... alas...

Pleasing temptation

Your branches beckon nearer

no danger greater—

I dangle closer

and make an uncomely splash.

(This poem originally appeared in *Mr. Sagittarius Poetry and Prose*)

Rainbow—Parasol of Light

Dear rainbow, so fine,

your colours reversed,

red on your inner-side arc,

double beauty, discovered.

Never leave me, dearest heart.

parasol of light, rainbow colours divine,

warming my soul, sweet route to inspiration,

hide me from pain and suffering.

Red, yellow, blue, indigo and violet,

many coloured dreams, such a beauty, shining joy.

Create with me, my rainbow friends.

(This poem originally appeared in *Mr. Sagittarius Poetry and Prose*)

Lollipop Sunshine Tree

Lollipop yellow

leaves fall in fragile raindrops

winter thoughts arrive.

Sweet autumn dissolving fast

leaving sunshine memories.

(This poem originally appeared in *Mr. Sagittarius Poetry and Prose*)

Section Two

Poems Inspired by Various Poets

The following poetry is inspired by poetry I've read by various poets, whose names I mention below each of my poems.

The Forest Weeps

This is the forest of my youth.

The trees so grand and towering.

Fearing nothing, feeling and hearing everything.

Each step, each cry, each breath, each touch.

The way ahead is illuminated by snatches of sun-lit kisses.

Cloaked moss creeping up tree trunks, green velveteen so soft to the touch,

The Druids merriment evident in their round jolly faces,

Their full bellies, and boisterous beards.

Now, many years later

The wind is whispering,

The leaves rustle and curl in protestation,

The birds pack up and go, taking their beloved nests with them.

The moment has come, the earth shudders,

As the proud trees and druids weep,

waiting for the first strike of the axe.

(Inspired by Henry Wadsworth Longfellow, *Evangeline*)

The Forest King

The forest king lives in the shadows,

his hair and beard, a flame alight,

in his crown, the fairy queen sits,

far from the tangled roots of his throne.

He, the king, sings the songs of the forest,

his bed's a branch from his old friend the tree,

his wondrous smile blesses all woodland folk,

and in his kingdom, his heart is his home.

If chance tempted you to kneel beside him,

would you take his weather-beaten hand?

To join in the sweet songs to be sung,

and cry with, and care for this land?

If your heart belongs here,

then you will be his dearest forest friend,

kneel beside him in tranquility,

in sweet silence, you will find a true hum of peace.

(Inspired by Ruby Archer, *King Forest*)

Raindrops and Childhood Dreams

Fast approaching,

wet feet running, summer rain,

first to reach that tree,

raindrops and childhood dreams.

Racing through the forest,

wet leaves squelching underfoot,

rain splattering on each tree trough to fill,

as plants thirst, quench to drink.

Dressed in robes of dress-up gold,

jewels sparkle as she runs,

with a breath of playful joy,

her slipper slips as she runs.

Clean fresh dew surrounds her,

the sun gleams like a god,

an Edenesque of old,

her lovely forest slipper rests.

(Inspired by Bliss Carman, *Woodland Rain*)

The Woodland Treasures

Who took the woodland treasures, and broke the trust and freedom to explore?

I know of no such wicked thing, this forest beauty must be free, unguarded.

Not his fantasy to steal!

He cast a magic cloak upon the forest jewels, hiding them at once; he whisked them all away.

In the whispers of the forest, who or what will bear the blame?

(Inspired by Emily Dickinson, *Who Robbed the Woods*)

Winter Woodland Moon

These woods belong to a squirrel friend of mine,

who lives in a treehouse up high,

he is sleeping now, eyes closed, he will not see,

me, amongst the snowy boughs in his winter canopy.

My friend the dog barks with curiosity,

at why I, a lone butterfly, ventures here, alone,

in this charming clearing of snow-filled trees,

with midnight moon for company.

(Inspired by Rupert Blake, *Stopping by The Woods on A Winter Evening*)

Child, Me

Bearing right at the woodland corner,

approaching the meadow's beginning,

brown feet, wide eyes,

I see you,

child—me.

Frolicking along, I hear your laughter,

trailing your beguiling memories with you,

and I pause, unable to decide,

who to follow—my memories, or my mischief?

Child me,

lasso me to those memories,

Child me,

sweet birdsong that almost forgotten laughter

spare me from this moonlight madness,

where this incantation of nostalgia alludes me.

(Inspired by Oscar Wilde, *In the Forest*)

REVIEWS

It is my dearest hope that you have enjoyed this poetry collection. If so, please do leave a review on sites such as Amazon, Goodreads, Bookbub, etc. Reviews mean so much to authors.

They don't have to be long... just a few words would do. Many thanks in anticipation, dearest readers.

ACKNOWLEDGEMENTS

To the writing, poetry, and blogging community—I owe you so much. Particular thanks to Colleen Chesebro for her continued enthusiasm, encouragement and kindness, inspiring me to write poetry and for including my poetry in her books: Word Weaving #1, a Word Craft Journal of Syllabic Verse: The Moons of Autumn: A Word Craft Journal of Syllabic Verse.

I also wish to thank Robbie Cheadle and Kaye Lynn Booth for publishing my poetry in the anthology, Poetry Treasures 2 Relationships: Wordcrafter Poetry Anthology.

To the wondrous Sisters of The Fey: Colleen Chesebro, Adele Marie Park, Debby Gies (D G Kaye,) Sally Cronin, and Annette Aben. Thank you for your help with beta editing, reviewing, supporting me, and sharing my work over the years.

ALSO, BY M J MALLON

Next Chapter Publishing

YA Fantasy series, The Curse of Time

For details of publications, please visit:

https://www.nextchapter.pub/authors/mj-mallon

Kyrosmagica Publishing

Poetry, Prose, and Photography: Mr. Sagittarius

http://mybook.to/MrSagittarius

Available on Amazon kindle, Kindle unlimited and paperback

Short Stories in Anthologies:

Bestselling horror compilations:

Nightmareland compiled by Dan Alatorre

"Scrabble Boy" (Short Story)

Spellbound compiled by Dan Alatorre

"The Twisted Sisters" (Short Story)

Wings of Fire compiled by Dan Alatorre

"The Great Pottoo" (Short Story)

Ghostly Rites 2019 compiled by Claire Plaisted"Dexter's Creepy Caverns" (Short Story)

Ghostly Rites 2020 compiled by Claire Plaisted

"No. 1 Coven Lane" (Short Story)

For all my publications and contributions to anthologies, please refer to my **Author Blog**: https://mjmallon.com

Amazon Author Page:
https://www.amazon.co.uk/M-J-Mallon/e/B074CGNK4L/

Twitter: @Marjorie_Mallon

GoodReads:
https://www.goodreads.com/author/show/17064826.M_J_Mallon

Facebook: https://www.facebook.com/mjmallonauthor/

Instagram: https://www.instagram.com/mjmallonauthor/

TikTok: https://www.tiktok.com/@mjmallonauthM J Mallon (@mjmallonauthor) TikTok | Watch M J Mallon's Newest TikTok Videos

Bookstagram: https://www.instagram.com/mjm_reviews/M J Mallon (Marjorie Mallon) (@mjm_reviews) • Instagram photos and videos

Bookbub: https://www.bookbub.com/authors/m-j-mallon

Authors, Bloggers Rainbow Support Club #ABRSC:
https://www.facebook.com/groups/1829166787333493/

ABOUT M J Mallon

My favourite genres to write are Fantasy YA, Paranormal, Ghost and Horror Stories, various forms of poetry and flash fiction. I celebrate the spiritual realm, love of nature and all things magical, mystical, and mysterious at my blog home: https://mjmallon.com

I'd describe myself as a reading, blogging and photography enthusiast!

 M J Mallon was born in Lion city Singapore, a passionate Scorpio with the Chinese Zodiac sign of a lucky rabbit. She spent her early childhood in Hong Kong. During her teen years, she returned to her father's childhood home, Edinburgh where she spent many happy years, entertained, and enthralled by her parents' vivid stories of living and working abroad. Perhaps it was during these formative years that her love of storytelling began bolstered by these vivid raconteurs. She counts herself lucky to have travelled to many far-flung destinations and this early wanderlust has fuelled her present desire to emigrate abroad. Until that wondrous moment, it's rumoured that she lives in the UK, in the Venice of Cambridge with her six-foot hunk of a rock god husband. Her two enchanting daughters have flown the nest but often return with a cheery smile.

I write fantasy/magical realism because life should be sprinkled with a liberal dash of extraordinarily imaginative magic! Her motto is to always do what you love, stay true to your heart's desires, and inspire others to do so too, even it if appears that the odds are stacked against you like black-hearted shadows.